HOOFEN FLOOFEN ISLAND

Lena Kay Rufus
and her mom, Monica J Sword

Illustrator
Lisa McGinley

Acknowledgements

It is uniquely gratifying to preserve the memory of my late daughter, Lena, through her story, *Hoofen Floofen Island*, which she wrote when she was just ten years old. Publishing any book has its joys and challenges. And in this case, love. Extraordinary love.

It is with utmost appreciation I honor the countless hours of time, expert advice, and unwavering belief in this project from these incredible people: Ron Smith, Lisa McGinley, Debra Marrs, Joey Meyers, Enrique Sanchez and, most especially, to Lena Kay Rufus (the ultimate muse).

And to you, dear readers, my gratitude for purchasing *Hoofen Floofen Island.* The proceeds from your book purchase benefit others through educational scholarships from the *Lena Kay Rufus Memorial Scholarship Fund* (see back cover for details).

May you experience wonder and delight in seeking new adventures, and may you enjoy the journey as much as the destination.

E
Ruf
pb

HO^OFEN FLO^OFEN ISLAND

Sword Smith Services, LLC

www.lifeisaprettyword.com

Publisher's Note: This is a work of fiction. Names, characters, businesses, places, and incidents are a product of the author's imagination with the exception of her own name. Any resemblance to actual people, living or dead, or actual events, is completely coincidental.

Artwork Styling: pen and ink, watercolor on 140 lb. hot pressed, extra white Fabriano Artistico paper

Lena Kay Rufus and Monica J Sword — First Edition

Illustrator: Lisa McGinley

Editor: Debra Marrs

Summary: Little Lena lives in the chilly and dark northland longing for sunshine when she wins a ticket to anywhere in the world.

ISBN 978-0-692-71848-3

Printed in the United States of America

For Lena

For my brave and darling daughter, Lena,
who taught me the meaning of love,
how to live fully, and who once asked herself,
"Do I really want to live this life?"
And then answered, *"I do."*
I do, too, Babe.

Lena Kay Rufus
November 1, 1980 - March 28, 2003

One gloomy day,

I won a ticket ...

to go anywhere I wanted in the whole world.

I could take a whole army
if I wanted to, but I didn't.

Instead, I took all my relatives,

my mom and dad,

and my whole class.

I wanted to seek new land.
So first we all packed up ...

and set sail ...

on the one and only
gross, cool ship!

Soon everyone
settled in,

and
everybody
was happy.

After one day
we spotted land.

Everybody was yelling,

"We're here!
We're here!"

Then my mom came forward
and said,
"Lena, you have traveled very far
and I'm proud of you."

"Now let's
    party!"

Everyone went ... surfing!

And
everywhere
you could hear
the laughs
of us.

Discussion Guide

Ask your child …

What are you most proud of?

Do you know why I'm proud of you?

Can you guess what the letters HFI stand for?

How many times does Lena's doggie appear?

Why do you think Lena named her story
Hoofen Floofen Island?

What or who makes you laugh?

What if you wrote a story?

Help your child write or draw a story …

What do your imaginary places look like?

What colors do you see?

What sounds do you hear?

Who will you take along?

How will you get there?

What might happen if you won a ticket?

What will you name your story?

CPSIA information can be obtained at www.ICGtesting.com
Printed in the USA
BVIW12n1041070717
488665BV00014B/255